W9-DEX-089

In the Diner

Written by Christine Loomis
Illustrated by Nancy Poydar

SCHOLASTIC INC.
New York

ISBN 0-590-46716-6

Library of Congress Catalog Card Number: 93-84594

12 11 10 9 8 7 6 5 4 3 2 1 4 5 6 7 8 9/9
Printed in the U.S.A. 37

First Scholastic printing, April 1994

For Kira,
whose unique approach
to food and
well-developed sense of
humor make her a fascinating
dining companion.

— C.L.

For elementary
school teachers, especially my
former colleagues.

— N.P.

Good Food
Smart Cat
JOE'S Big Fish
Please No Smoking

In the diner ...

Waiters hurry.

Busboys scurry.

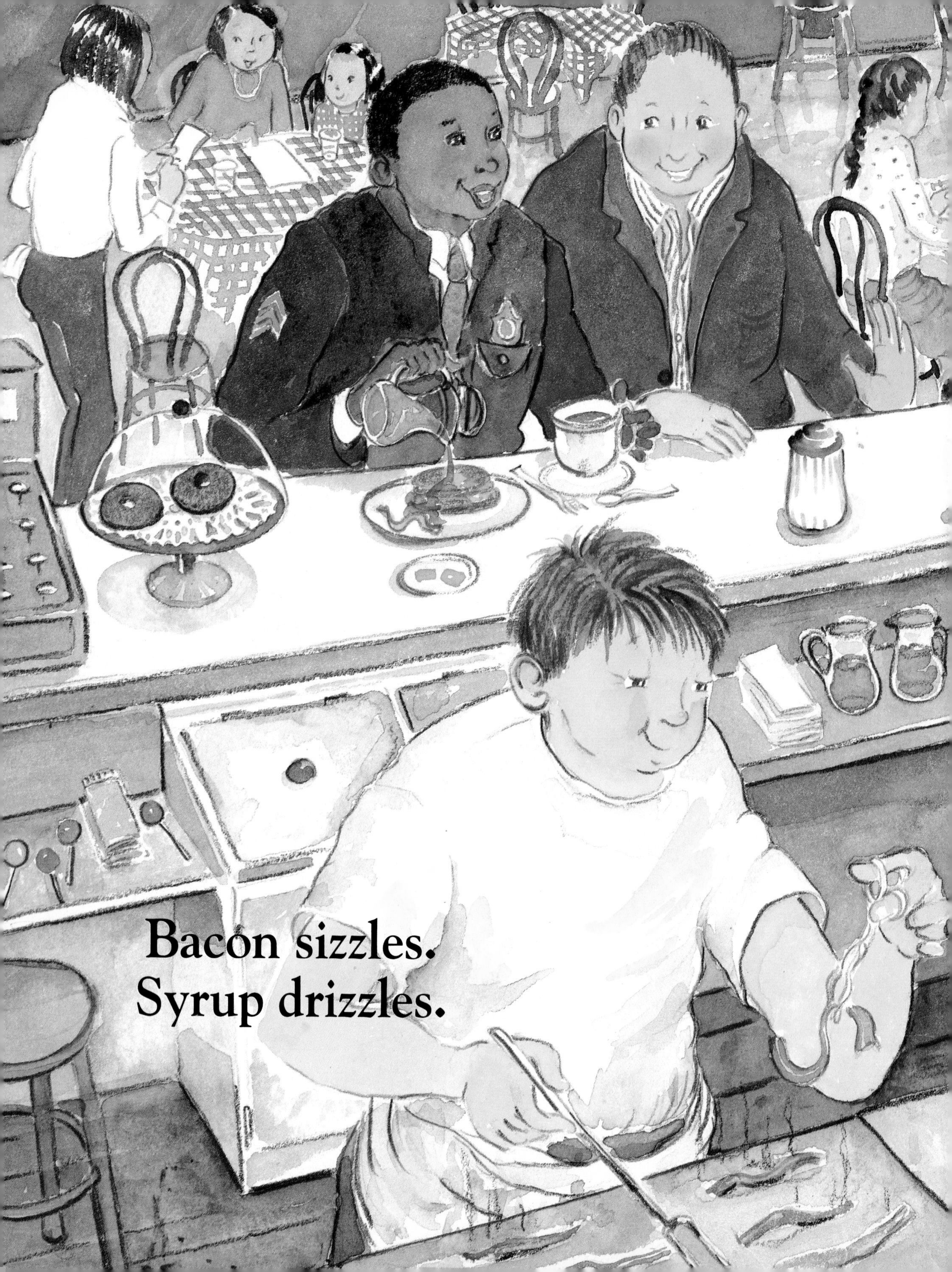

Bacon sizzles.
Syrup drizzles.

Coffee brews.
Beef stews.

Bagels toast.
Turkeys roast.

Soap bubbles.
Dough doubles.

Baker stirs.
Cat purrs.

Cook flips.
Scale tips.

Cake bakes.

Cat wakes.

Burgers broil.
Sauces boil.

Fish grills.
Gravy spills.

Hostess greets.

Crowd eats.

Girl hides.

Dog guides.

Platters clatter.
People chatter.

Stool twirls.

Chocolate swirls!

Ice cream freezes.
Someone sneezes.

Boy slurps.
Baby burps.

Waiters stack.
Cups crack.

Saucers clunk.
Washers dunk.

People pay.
It's a day

… in the diner.

EDISON TWP. FREE PUBLIC LIBRARY
3 9360 00328773 0